Swimming Sal

Written by Carol Molski

Illustrated by Mary Newell DePalma

Eerdmans Books for Young Readers

Grand Rapids, Michigan ❂ Cambridge, U.K.

Published in 2009 by Eerdmans Books for Young Readers
an imprint of Wm. B. Eerdmans Publishing Co.

Wm. B. Eerdmans Publishing Co.
2140 Oak Industrial Dr. NE
Grand Rapids, Michigan 49505
P.O. Box 163, Cambridge CB3 9PU U.K.

www.eerdmans.com/youngreaders

Manufactured in China

14 13 12 11 10 09   9 8 7 6 5 4 3 2 1

Library of Congress Cataloging-in-Publication Data

Molski, Carol.
Swimming Sal / by Carol Molski ; illustrated by Mary Newell DePalma.
p. cm.
Summary: As the only dog at Hilltop Farm who has never won an award, Sal,
encouraged by her mother's reminder of her Portuguese water dog heritage,
decides to perfect her swimming skills by joining the swim team at the YMCA.

ISBN 978-0-8028-5327-1 (alk. paper)

[1. Dogs — Fiction. 2. Swimming — Fiction. 3. Farm life — Fiction.
4. Humorous stories.] I. DePalma, Mary Newell, ill. II. Title.
PZ7.M73536Sw 2009
[E] — dc22   2008009996

Display type created by Mary Newell DePalma
Text type set in ITC Quorum BT
Illustrations created with acrylics on watercolor paper

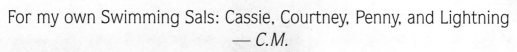

For my own Swimming Sals: Cassie, Courtney, Penny, and Lightning
— *C.M.*

For Meredith and Janie
— *M.N.D.*

Every dog at Hilltop Farm was a winner.

Penny won medals in the agility contests.

Buster won trophies
for sheepherding.

And Sadie won ribbons for
Best of Show.

Every dog at Hilltop Farm was a winner —
every dog except Sal.

Sal couldn't jump hurdles.
Her legs were too short.
She couldn't herd sheep.
It gave her a woolly mouth.
And her nose was too flat
to win Best of Show.

Poor Sal!

Sal was good at only one thing — swimming!

She swam in the creek behind the house.

She swam in her plastic pool.

She even swam in the bathtub.

But nobody gave out medals to a swimming dog.

"Don't worry, Sal," her mother would say.
"You're just a wag from your mother's tail.
It's that little bit of Portuguese Water Dog in you.
Someday you'll be Swimming Sal,
the Swimmingest Dog in the World."

So Sal swam every day.
Stroke. Stroke.
"I'm a wag from my mother's tail," she would say to herself.
Stroke. Stroke.

But Sal wanted more.
She wanted a medal to add to the
other medals at Hilltop Farm.
She wanted to be Swimming Sal,
the Swimmingest Dog in the World.

If only she could do more than the doggy paddle.
She wanted to learn the backstroke
and the breaststroke.
She wanted to learn the butterfly
and the front crawl.

Sal thought.
She thought some more.

She thought
as she did the dead dog's float
in the creek behind the house.

She thought
as she practiced kicking in the bathtub.

And she thought
as she practiced diving into
her plastic pool.

Finally Sal came up with a plan.
She would join the local swim team!

Sal waited for the next practice.
She crawled into Annie's gym bag
and was carried to the locker room.

Sal crawled out of the bag and
joined the line of swimmers.
The children looked at her.
They giggled and laughed.
"Are you going to learn how to swim?"
they asked.
Sal wagged her tail.

"Don't tell Coach Mary,"
they whispered to each other.

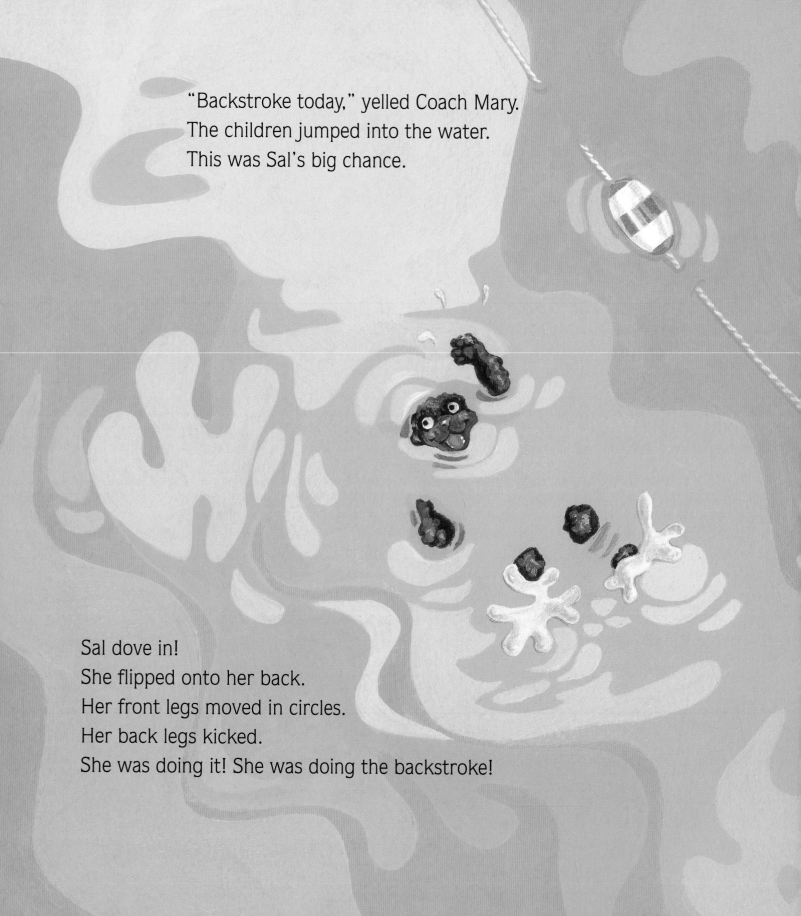

"Backstroke today," yelled Coach Mary.
The children jumped into the water.
This was Sal's big chance.

Sal dove in!
She flipped onto her back.
Her front legs moved in circles.
Her back legs kicked.
She was doing it! She was doing the backstroke!

Sal joined the swimmers at the pool.

The swimmers were working on the front crawl.
Sal jumped into the water.
She moved her front legs in circles.
She kicked her back legs.

Sal swam fast, then faster.
Soon she was just a blur in the water.
Stroke. Stroke.
"I'm a wag from my mother's tail."
Stroke. Stroke.

The teeny tiny bikini began to slip.
It slipped around Sal's tail and hung like a flag.

Sal let out a yelp of excitement.
Coach Mary looked in the water.
"Dog in the pool!" she yelled.
"Everybody out!"

Poor Sal! What would she do?

Sal hid in the locker room.
"Time for Plan B,"
she thought.

She looked in a locker and
found what she needed —
the perfect disguise!

Coach Mary looked at the flag in the water.
"Dog in the pool!" she yelled. "Everybody out!"

"Busted again!" thought Sal.
She tucked her tail between her legs and slowly walked home.

Coach Mary hung a sign on the gate.

Sal had to learn how to swim.
She had to win a medal for Hilltop Farm.
She had to be Swimming Sal,
the Swimmingest Dog in the World.

Sal thought.
She thought some more.

She thought
as she practiced holding her breath
in the creek behind the house.

She thought
as she did flip turns
in her little plastic pool.

And she thought
as she did the sidestroke
in the bathtub.

But Sal could not come up with a plan.
"Maybe I'm not a wag from my mother's tail
after all," she thought. "Maybe I'm just Silly Sal,
the Silliest Dog in the World."

Sal walked slowly to the local pool.
A big swim meet was going on.
She watched through the fence.

It was time for the big relay race.
The first swimmer ran to the block.
WHOOSH!
She slipped on the wet floor and hurt her ankle.

Oh no! The relay team did not have enough swimmers now!
What would they do?

This was Sal's big chance!
She rushed through the gate.
She grabbed a swim cap.
She grabbed a pair of goggles.

Sal was ready to swim!

"We'll give it a try," said Coach Mary.

BANG! The starting gun went off.

Annie swam the backstroke.
Kick. Kick. Kick.
Stroke. Stroke. Stroke.
The other team was in the lead!

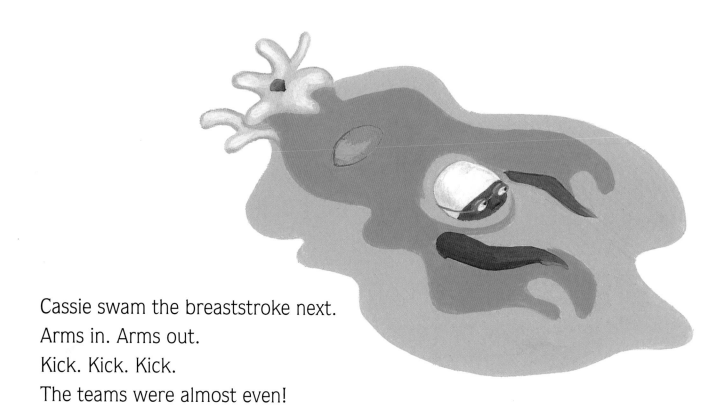

Cassie swam the breaststroke next.
Arms in. Arms out.
Kick. Kick. Kick.
The teams were almost even!

Then Courtney swam the butterfly.
The two teams were neck and neck!

Finally, it was Sal's turn to swim.
She dove into the water.
She did her best stroke — the doggy paddle.

Sal swam fast. And faster.
Stroke. Stroke.
"I'm a wag from my mother's tail."
Stroke. Stroke.

Sal was in the lead!
The crowd went wild.
"Go, Sal, go!" they yelled.

Sal moved her legs faster.
Her front paws touched the wall.
Sal had won the race!
The crowd cheered.
Sal had saved the day!

Coach Mary placed a medal around Sal's neck.
Sal had won first place.
Hilltop Farm had another winner.

"I *am* a wag from my mother's tail," Sal thought.
"I'm Swimming Sal, the Swimmingest Dog in the World."